This book is dedicated to my
beautiful wife Sharon and
our three amazing children,
Ava, Jack and Jordon. — K.H.

For my favorite little pickles, Will,
Elizabeth, Edward and Charlotte. — K.C.

Text copyright © 2016 by Kenny Herzog
Illustrations copyright © 2016 by Kelly Canby

First edition 2016

Published by Peter Pauper Press, Inc.
202 Mamaroneck Avenue
White Plains, New York 10601
U.S.A.

Published in the United Kingdom and Europe by Peter Pauper Press, Inc.
c/o White Pebble International
Unit 2, Plot 11 Terminus Rd.
Chichester, West Sussex PO19 8TX, UK

Library of Congress Cataloging-in-Publication Data Available

ISBN 978-1-4413-1933-3
Manufactured for Peter Pauper Press, Inc.
Printed in Hong Kong

7 6 5 4 3 2 1

Visit us at www.peterpauper.com

Phil PICKLE

by KENNY HERZOG

Illustrated by Kelly Canby

 PETER PAUPER PRESS, INC.
WHITE PLAINS, NEW YORK

Phil Pickle lived in a pickle jar.
And was meant to share the
same fate as all the other
pickles he lived with.

"Next to a
burger and fries
on a plate," Helen Pickle always said.

(Helen was one of the many
pickles floating above Phil's head.)

"But I want to be an ACTOR," Phil told them all.

He'd felt this way ever since he heard two shoppers
talking about a movie where a man dressed up
like a woman, just to get a role in a soap opera.

"I want to pretend to be different characters
with unique and interesting lives," Phil explained.

"You know how many pickle actors there are out there? **NONE. ZERO.** zilch," one of the sour pickles chimed in.
"Not even on off-off Broadway!" said another.

"Think what you want, but it just so happens that I have an audition at a casting company in the city at 2:55," Phil said.

"Why not 3:00?" Moishe Pickle, a kosher pickle, asked.

"2:55 is what my agent said to me. It's very organized in show biz," replied Phil.

Although the sour pickles did not believe him, Phil actually _did_ have an audition that day.

It was for a laundry detergent commercial. When Phil arrived, he couldn't believe how many actors were in the waiting area.

"Like pickles in a jar," he thought to himself, shaking his head,

"just like pickles in a _jar_."

"It's Phil PICKLE, not Prickle," Phil Pickle said.

It was too late to escape.

He followed the man inside.

As he walked, his feet felt like cement blocks.

"What was I thinking?" he thought to himself.

"I can't act.

I'm nothing but a glorified

CONDIMENT."

When he walked inside the studio, the director and everyone else stared at him quizzically.

Then, after a shrug, the director started speaking.

"Thanks for coming in. Your dialogue is on these cue cards. Amy here will be reading with you. And please, don't ham it up," the director said.

"I actually go pretty well with **ham**. He-heh," Phil said to break the ice.

But no one laughed.
He felt the need to explain the joke, but thought better of it.
Instead he just cleared his throat.

Then the director took a sip of his coffee and a bite of a brownie, and with a mouth full of chocolate, called out, "ACTION!"

When the director opened his mouth, Phil noticed he had some brownie stuck in his teeth.
And because it made the director look silly, it made Phil relax.

So Phil took a deep breath and bellowed the first line of dialogue from the script.

"Martha, bad news. I got mud stains on my favorite shirt. The one I was going to wear to my job interview."

the director shouted.

"It felt like you were a little too upset. Too dramatic. It's just a mud stain on a shirt. It's not like you had to flush your goldfish down the toilet.

Be upset about the stain, but in a more realistic way."

Phil listened to the director's feedback, and did another take. The director seemed pleased and asked him to try it again.

This time after saying his line, Phil threw his shirt on the floor—something he ad-libbed.

Everyone in the room seemed excited so he kept going. Phil felt like he was on a roll, but all of a sudden, the director yelled...

"Next actor!"

Phil was crushed.

He felt like he'd been run through a deli slicer.

He rushed out of the room as fast as he could, forgetting to thank the panel for the opportunity to audition.

It didn't matter.

He just wanted
to get back to
the comfort of
his pickle juice.

When he got back to the jar,
he was mobbed by the other pickles—
all asking questions about the audition.

"I suppose," said Phil, fighting back briny tears.

As he looked away from the other pickles, he saw a big pair of googly eyes peering through the jar.

At first he thought it was a shopper, but then realized it was his agent.

"Elaine. What are you doing here?" asked Phil.

"I heard back from the casting company," she said.

Phil could feel his heart beating.
He could also feel the stares of every pickle
in every jar in the entire aisle.
Some watched so intently that
their faces were smushed up
against the front of the jars.

"They decided to go with an actor named...

Phil Pickle!

You just booked a national spot," Elaine exclaimed.

"shooting starts next Tuesday."

"...Oh, and before I go, one more thing. Can you tell me where the pasta aisle is?"

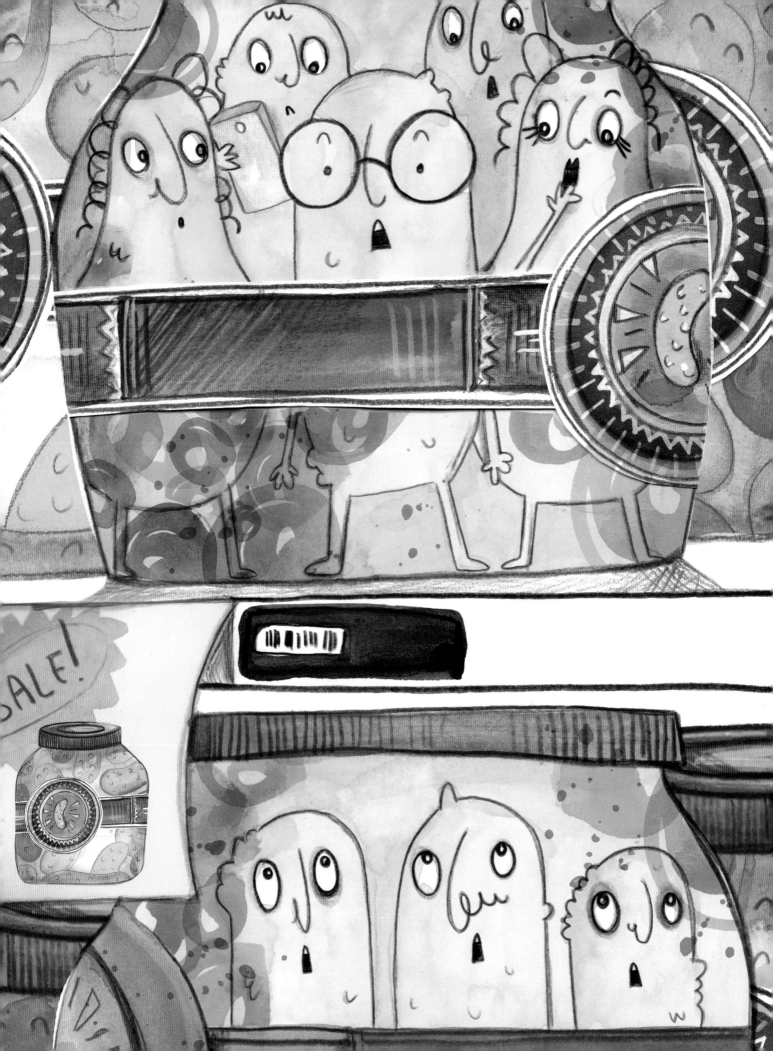

But Phil couldn't answer.

He was too much in shock—
as was every other
pickle in the jar.

Except for Henry, who missed the news
because he was too busy playing
Angry Dills on his phone.

Before Phil's agent left the store,
she swung by the condiment aisle
one more time to tell Phil about
an upcoming audition for a
car commercial.

"Well, the script better be good,"

Phil said as he winked, making it clear he only said it in jest. He planned to stay humble despite his success.

The news quickly spread and Phil was the talk of the entire grocery store. All of the pickles were so happy for him.
But it was more than that.
He became an inspiration to pickles everywhere.

... not even those sour pickles doubted her.